Persian Nights

Persian Ratri

NK Mondal

ISBN 978-93-5610-455-6

Published in India 2022 by Pencil

A brand of
One Point Six Technologies Pvt. Ltd.
123, Building J2, Shram Seva Premises,
Wadala Truck Terminal, Wadala (E)
Mumbai 400037, Maharashtra, INDIA
E connect@thepencilapp.com
W www.thepencilapp.com

Author biography

NK Mondal (Hindi: एन.के.मंडल) is an indian poet,writer, social adviser, script writer, columnist, and novelist from the state of West bengal, India.He is also a writer.He was awarded with the title of Sahitya Ratna in 2019. And he former member of West bengal Intelligence Committee from Murshidabad,India.Mondal was born on 5 may 1996 from Murshidabad district in India.His parents Saiful Shaikh and Menuka Bibi used to lovingly call him Salim.He passed higher secondary examination from Rukanpur High School, Murshidabad.He earned degree in bachelor of arts from Hazi A.K.Khan College, University of Kalyni.

CONTENTS

Iranian Nights 1

Akash is a handsome muscular strong rich young man. She is newly married. The wife's name is Alo. As beautiful as she looks, so beautiful is the mind. She is like the princess of Rupnagar. However, the shy and story-crazy girl. Alo may even sit up all night without listening to the story. That's why she married the storyteller boy. I want his story to be heard every night. Moreover, the newlyweds will rejoice. Akash gets angry if he can't tell a story with fun. Akash said jokingly one day, I can't tell a story anymore. Besides, you are not a child. It will burst. Akash got angry in the morning light but left the office. He came back from the office in the afternoon and saw that the light was still on. Akash went to the light and said, O queen of my heart, you are still angry. I'm sorry. Today I'll tell you a story you've never heard. Alo smiled and said, really. Yes go Go hungry Prepare food for two. Saying this, Alo took Akash's hand and said with a smile, let's eat. Akash said calmly in his mind, crazy girl.

The first night

After the two have eaten, Alo is sitting on the bed with a pillow on the wall of the bed. And Akash put his head on the thigh of light and started telling stories. Billy is cutting the hair of the light sky.

So listen, there was a handsome and intelligent adult brave boy in Sudan. Children of poor families. Eats day after day. In a needy family, father is the only hope. So his mother called Bashar al-Assad, the only son, that handsome and brave boy, and said, "Father Ashad, bring flour from the grocery store for these two rupees." Bread has to be made. Assad said, "All right." Mom, give me the money. On the way to the grocery store, Assad's best friend and only lover called. She was Nayana. Then Alo said, who is Nayana. Nayana is the lover of Bashar al-Assad. Alo said, well tell me now.

Nayana is a beautiful young woman's body has a lot of sensual irritation. One day Assad is walking to school. And Nayana is going backwards on the bicycle. Assad looked back and immediately smiled. Because there is a little weakness towards Assad. He longed for Assad. Assad knew that, but he did not say anything. Nayana said from behind, Bose got on the back of the bicycle. It took about half an hour to cross half the jungle of the village. Nayana repeatedly tells Assad to get to school, It is as if he were sitting on the edge of the forest near the forest. Because the touch of Assad's hand plays electricity on his body. White and pink tights fitting dress would fall. Many times he would let Assad ride his bicycle and he would sit on Assad's waist. But Assad could not ride a bicycle for long. Seeing Nayana's body, many people's bodies would get irritated. Even Assad. Many in the school could not see Assad because he was looking at him. He got into trouble with many. Couldn't bear to say anything about the eyes. At that time, the light said, Nayana was Assad's lover. Yes he had a girlfriend. Akash started telling stories again. I don't love Assad very much. Nayana was Assad's lover. Yes he had a girlfriend. Akash started telling stories again. I don't love Assad very much. Nayana was Assad's lover. Yes he had a girlfriend. Akash started telling stories again. I don't love Assad very much.

One day Asad and Nayana are sitting on the roof of Nayana. While sitting and talking, Nayana said, well, he was really talking. What's up Do you love me Assad heard this and disappeared. He said nothing more. Nayana then said, I know the answer to this. How much you love me Saying this, holding Assad's hands, he is slowly pulling Assad towards himself. Even then, there is no word on Assad's face. It seems to have killed the glue. Then Nayana says to Assad, I love you Assad. How long will I wait for you? I can't anymore. Give me a little caress. He pulled Assad to his chest and hugged him. And hugged. He grabbed Assad's hands and held his waist. Telling her to grip her waist with a wink. Nayana Maja began to kiss her forehead and lips vigorously. Assad unbuttoned his shirt. Filling all the organs of the body with kisses, Even then, Assad's heart is pounding with excitement. But no words are coming out of his mouth. In the same way, Nayana is watching who is eating him like a ferocious tiger. After spending some time with Assad, the two of them came down to Nayana's bed.

He came down and sat on the sofa. Even then, Assad's body is sweating profusely. All the clothes are soaking wet. Nayana turned on the ceiling fan at high speed and went to another room. After a while, Nayana brought the fruit juice to the plate, beef and thin hot rice bread and served it in front of him. Assad ate everything he could because he was hungry and hungry. By then Assad's wet clothes had dried in the air. Nayana finally led Assad to the main gate of the house.

The second night

The story of the second night began again. Akash Alo both of them sat on the bed with pillows. And for today's story telling and listening. Akash started telling stories.

Listen, Assad's mother paid for the flour. As soon as Assad was going to buy flour, Nayana called out. Assad can't take his eyes off him. So Nayana left the matter of buying flour and went to go to the haystack again. The two fell into a haystack. And Nayana says today you have to caress the most and right now. Assad disagrees, saying his mother sent him to the grocery store to buy flour. She did not listen to him and started playing her sex game with Assad. At the end of the game, Nayana lovingly gifted him a waterproof watch. And he put it in his hand. And he said forgive me if you can.

I am leaving the village. Father's transfer. But you be good. I will never find a sex partner like you anywhere in my life. Forgive me Chris Ray says, Nayana ran away crying. Assad ran but could not. Assad suffered a sudden chest pain. He forgot to buy flour and was walking up the nearby hill. Assad rolled over and fell into a ditch as he fell to the ground. After a while he woke up and saw that he was unconscious. He could not get up even after trying a thousand times. After wandering around for a while, I saw A door. Assad entered through the gate. The gate closed as soon as he entered. At that time Akash's mother brought coffee for Akash and Alo. After receiving the coffee from his mother, he thanked her and Akash's mother went inside the house to tell them the story. He wanted the sky and the light. For the time being, he stopped telling stories like that day, and the two of them started laughing and joking.

The third night

Listen, then the photo stopped. Assad got a little frightened. Then Assad started walking on a narrow road. Another road was found on a rock. The torch was burning, so he thought that there must be a human connection. I liked it and took it in many pockets. Going forward I saw a big photo again. The gate can be seen without torch light. I came to the gate and saw that there is no lock key to open the photo.

Tried many times but couldn't. Assad is tired. Then he thought that it would be better to try to return home. But the question arose in his mind, what is the secret here. Mysterious cave here. So he decided that whatever happened, he would have to unravel the mystery of this cave. At that time he saw that Akash was getting a deep sleep while telling stories. Listening to the light lying down. It was eleven o'clock at night. The light is meant to indicate something with the gesture of the eyes. I mean. Seeing the sky stop telling stories, There has been some cum excitement in the light. And that's how the costumes are different from this evening. Tight fitting light thin pink dress to attract men. Medium pajamas. Looks pretty good. The breasts are swollen and beautiful. Akash did not notice that. After seeing the sky, he could not hold himself. Then the newly-married man began to tickle his hands and feet with a stick on his stomach and back. Raised above the navel. Kissing is filling the kiss with light. The light falls on the bed and it is humming softly as well as the breasts are puffing. The two of them are pressing their hands together. Akash leaned back in bed after a long day of activities.

Fourth night

The story of the fourth night began

Assad is walking towards the gate. Can't find any clues. As he walked, his eyes suddenly went to the head of the gate or over the door. There was a two-line sentence. The door opened as I read the sentence from beginning to end. What a joy for Assad then. The torch is burning inside. Light dark. The door closed as I read the sentence a second time. The door opened to read the sentence again. And began to walk side by side. Walking, it was seen that the skeletons of dead people were scattered. Assad paused. I was shocked.

Then Assad's body is dripping with sweat. The water is falling. Light trembling. Trembling, he slowly moved towards the skeleton. He is holding a torch in his left hand. As we approached the skeleton, we saw a huge locket. Maybe iron or some other metal. The locket is gleaming in the torchlight as it rubs against the fallen stone. Began to flicker.

Then it became clear that it was made of a precious metal. When he saw the locket, it fell from his hand and became two halves. A small piece of paper was found in the locket. And the map has some more writing and design given. Assad folded the paper as usual and put it in his pocket. If it ever comes in handy. Assad started walking again with the locket. Light light dark. Occasionally torches are burning on both sides of the road. Finally came to a room. The house is round or round. There are many similar roads in this house. He also lost the way he entered. It is not too late for Assad to realize that this is a maze. Getting out of here is not easy.

Going to the streets one by one. But arriving at that round house. Similar incidents are happening again and again. Assad's head began to ache. Still trying to control himself. I am very hungry. The body is looking weak. Got thirsty for water. He kept thinking about how to get out of here. The breath is coming off. Assad wants to cry. Then he is consoling himself that he should not be afraid, he should have courage. After a while, an idea came to Assad's head. Wisdom to aim the way with shiny stones in the pocket. Just like thinking works. Each road is marked with a stone. And keep walking. Eventually there are two ways to go, one is the outer way and the other is the inner way. Assad did not come out, but walked in to unravel the mystery. The light is walking in the dark. Just when the torch is burning in the hand, Suddenly the torch is shaking. Then Assad thinks the way has been found. The wind is blowing in the empty space. That is why the torch is trembling. A little walk to see the empty field. As well as the weather. Assad dropped the torch and lay down on the empty ground. And the green-green grass fell asleep. There are various orchards of acacia, date, mango, lemon etc. There are also various flower gardens and trees all around. The mind will be fascinated by that. He woke up and began to cry, then his body was strong, but Don was sitting in the stomach with a needle in his stomach. While walking, I picked some raw ripe fruits and ate them. And he drank water from the nearby river and worshiped his stomach. Assad saw well that this was an empty space. Just a green field as far as the eye can see. Occasionally plants. A very quiet place. And in the distance a palace can be seen. Assad was shocked to see this. And there are big hills around the empty space that you see. That's when I realized, hey, This is no other place. It is a mountain valley. But such a large valley. All the empty space is filled with half a handful of weeds. Next to it are various kinds of flowers and fruit trees. Sometimes all the trees are planted like Zhou tree.

Breeze and pleasant atmosphere all the time. Neither cold nor hot. Such a place seemed to Assad, As if he had gone to heaven. But the surprising thing is that there are no human beings. Or people. There is no human existence. Assad is walking along the river bank by another road without going to the palace road. It goes without saying that there is no water in the river. There is little water. There is one knee amount of water. Good water is flowing. Lots of different kinds of fish are playing. I was upset to see the fish to catch. The mind is fidgeting but there is nothing to do. That is why Assad has been singing over and over again without noticing it. At that time, a stone statue was seen sitting by the river with a spear in the shape of a fish. He took the spear and caught some water insects and threw the spear into the river. Within minutes a big fish was caught. As soon as the fish was caught, an intelligence played in Assad's head. He chopped off the twigs and leaves of the dried tree and rubbed the stone to burn the fish. But then there is Assad's house and fear

Akash saw that the light had fallen asleep while telling the story. It feels cold to get a little rain today. Akash covered her body with a sheet.

Iranian Nights 2

After taking some rest after eating burnt fish, he started walking. Walking towards the palace. The streets of the palace are paved. Assad finally reached the main gate of the palace on foot. No, there is no sepoy or guard. Absolutely Shunshan. There is no one around the gate. People are nothing but animals. Assad kept saying, "What kind of place is this, father?" Slowly began to enter with fear. The main gate was open. Crossed and saw all the beautiful animals and birds. And surprisingly, there are idols of humans and monsters. Suddenly looking through the rooms of all the palaces, he saw through a window that, A room is furnished with a variety of food items. Polao-biryani kebabs and a variety of fruits. Colorful wine juices contain as much food as desired. Which Assad has never seen in his life. He is eating slowly without rushing. Kalia meat of rice fish and various kinds of fruits and juices. After finishing the meal, he started walking from one room to another again. But no one is anywhere. As he was walking, he saw the door of a room open and entered. And was surprised to enter the room. A sick man was found in this uninhabited place. The man is tied with an iron chain in a light worn out emaciated state. Assad was shocked and stunned. Assad called out several times, but the answer came in a soft voice. Water. With everything inside the room, he took a bottle of water and grabbed the old man. The old man untied the chain before he could say anything. He slowly He sat up and thanked Assad. Assad told the sick man,

Uncle, why are you in this condition? And who owns this Shunshan Palace. The old man said talking about me. Tell me your identity first.

I am a student. And I am a child of a poor family. And told the story of his life. All spoke of the cave. The old man then said, what is the name of your country. My country's name is Sudan. This is a country I do not know. There are one hundred and eighty countries in the world. Maybe you don't know and it has been independent for some years. The old has taken over the new sultan. Then the old man said I have memorized the map and I understand it. The old man is explaining that. But Assad does not understand. Even the clock does not match. After a long time, it occurred to the old man that there was magic in this palace. External information will be noisy. It is difficult to understand until the magic is free. Then the old man began to speak magic and the old man began to speak his own words.

Listen Dad, I'm the only powerful king in the land of Venus. My country will not be able to defeat my country even if 10 countries fight together. Suddenly Assad asked another question, "Well, why don't you have any human beings or creatures in this palace?" The Sultan then said, "This is not my palace." It is the palace of robbers and sorcerers. A man comes to this palace to give me light water and food. And the bandits come to beat me one day a week. Assad then asked why he was beating you. The old king then says, then listen to my history.

Listen, I am very popular with the people of the country. And my subjects respect and love me like a god. I was always on the side of various small and big problems of the people. Prajadardi learned from my father to get proper justice. Father's only child. So I got the throne right after my father. My current life was about 55 plus age. One day I was traveling without troops on the banks of the river Suvia. Because I do not have or did not have such an enemy in my country. But that is what happened to me. Suddenly a band of robbers and magicians came and attacked me. Bring me to this palace in a moment. And when I come here, I see my future son-in-law or future son-in-law. There is with them. In the middle of the story, Assad said, why would your future son-in-law do that. He is your son-in-law. Then listen, Dad.

One day I was discussing with Begum at home that our princess has become an adult and it is time to get married. Begum agreed and said, "Of course I told Begum that if the princess had any choice, she could bring him before me." As the princess was listening from outside the room, Begum told the princess. Whether he has that choice. A few days later a guard went to the court and said that a guest had come. I went to Begum's room and saw her. Begum, Shahjadi and a boy are sitting. I quickly realized that this was the princess's favorite boy. As soon as I entered the room, he greeted me. After gossiping for a while, I prayed for them. And I said I have no objection to you. The princess hugged and caressed me. I put my hand on the girl's head and assured her. Time goes on like this.

Sixth night

One day I announced that my heir to the throne after me, my worthy heir, my youngest son Mohammad Aziz will sit on the throne. From this announcement I began to conspire unknowingly. How to remove Prince Mohammad Aziz. After a while, the son-in-law said in a word, how can a little prince get a throne if he has a big prince. The son-in-law did not get a chance to talk to me. And I entered my room in thought.

After a long time, suddenly Prince Mohammad Aziz is not available. It has been getting dark since morning but he did not come to the palace. I told my eldest son and son-in-law to keep searching without the knowledge of the people of the country. But they went in front of the people and made a story about the disappearance of the prince and started promoting me as the king of failure. They preached that a king who could not handle his son could be called a failure king. And the people say that if the king cannot control his own son, then what will happen to the people like you. Many tenants believed and many tenants did not believe it. They believed in me that our king was not like that. He also spread rumors against me without my knowledge.

I will find out much later. But then the eldest son and son-in-law fled to a secret dormitory. A large number of soldiers and feudal lords conducted a search but to no avail. A few days later a letter came there demanding ransom. They both want to be Nawabs of two states. I wanted to give it to them. My body is slowly deteriorating. It is difficult to run the country. That is why I put Princess Ileana on the throne.

As a temporary ruler. The princess began to hate her son-in-law for his dishonesty. And properly carried out his rule or responsibilities. The prince is searching. I wanted to pay the ransom. I told the prince to give them two kingdoms. For now, let the prince return to the palace. The princess will be ready to pay the ransom in a few days. At that time one day the prince fled to the palace in disguise. There or a woman left him in love. Princess Ileana's army fled with the feudal lords, but a search turned up nothing. They had already fled.

Then Assad said to the old man, "Uncle, now I understand that they brought you here and cast a spell on you." Fear of not going anywhere and how long I have been chained, this is my short story.

Akash didn't tell the story anymore and said it will happen again tomorrow if he falls asleep saying inshallah. Alo fell asleep with her head on Akash's chest. Today she had sex but Akash fell asleep earlier so Alo didn't bother her husband anymore.

Seventh night

I was very upset to hear the biography of Asad Sultan. The locket suddenly fell out of Assad's chest pocket and that is what caught the king's eye. The king said, "Where did you get this locket?" The king spoke about the skeleton of the cave and all the words.

When the king heard this, he wept bitterly. That is my cousin. And the locket is no ordinary locket. My cousin Sultan Salauddin has a secret treasury design. At that moment, Assad asked if Sultan Salahuddin was away from you. We need to know something about him. If not, how do I understand the design. The king said, "Then listen."

One day laughter is going on in the court. There was no work that day. So the clown of the court was intoxicated with the story. In such a situation an envoy arrived. He came to the court and greeted me and said, "Sultan Salauddin has greeted you." He sent a message for you. The messenger sent me a message and went to the guest house. The letter said,

Hi. My dear brother. I know you must be fine. The family is fine. But I'm not good. The administration is being disrupted. I'm very worried. My request is that you come with the messenger. This is my request to you. This is your big brother. I am the king of the country.

I consulted with Begum and left with the envoy. It took

two days to ride a camel in the desert. I had 40 soldiers with me. We reached the capital two days later. Sultan Salauddin greeted us in advance and took us to the palace. That is my cousin. He hugged her and cried. He finally took me to his private room. The khas for the soldiers has been taken to the guest house. There are various kinds of royal food poured in front of me. The palace seemed to be filled with laughter and joy. The day went well into the night.

The next afternoon my older brother took me for a walk in a royal park. Maybe or something he will say personally. He asked me to sit on an open stone sofa and the Sultan himself sat down. Then he said to me, I have brought you here to speak privately. That's what I thought at first. Brought here for his personal talk. I agreed to talk to my older brother. He started telling me.

Sultan Salahuddin said, "Listen, my dear little brother." I'm old There is no heir. It is not possible for me to run the country. So I decided that what I really needed to do was learn how to do it right. King Aziz said, "No, big brother, I can't do that." I don't want any more greed. Sultan Salahuddin said, "Look, my younger brother." I am in great danger. Many in the country are secretly hostile. King Aziz said he would be seen later.

I calmed my elder brother a little and came to the palace. Big brother takes me here and there. A few days passed quite well. A few days later I left with everything ready to come to Venice. Venus or Qiyam is another name for the kingdom of King Aziz. My older brother gave me a

locket like this before. And spoke of mystery. What's the secret in this locket? Asad asked the king while listening to the story of Sultan Salahuddin. What is in this locket? King Aziz said,
Then listen to that story.

This locket has an engraved map design which is the treasury of Sultan Salauddin's secret treasure. Whose address no one knows except him. And he knows the only locket. Because it contains the address of all travel. Big brother gave me one and he had one. I left the country I bought and 14 days later a news came to my court. The chief commander of the Vizion has joined hands with the bandits to seize the throne. The nephew may have wanted to tell me this but I didn't understand. Where has the nephew Sultan Salauddin gone missing? My soldiers searched in disguise but could not find out. I'm scrambling to rescue my nephew. I was thinking of dealing with the purchase and possession of son-in-law together in a few days. I was not feeling well so I was traveling on the banks of the river Suvia without any companions. That's when he brought me here. I have already informed you about this. I understand now They are all a group. It must be avenged. I have to escape from here. And you can set me free.

At that moment, Assad said, "You are under the spell of magic." King Aziz said, "It is possible for you to do that." Not for me. You say the way I will do it, anyway inshaAllah. King Aziz said, listen and how it will work.

First you have to get out of this palace. After going out, you will see a stone statue by the river. The spear is stuck in the hand. At that moment there is a fountain of water in his head. The water of that fountain will be released only after feeding me. But it is not usually a fountain. That's a magic fountain. You can't see the water falling. If you want to take water, you can see the idol by turning it twice to the right. There you will find a staircase. You have to go down the stairs. And Patalpuri will get. There is a fountain there. If you drink the water of that fountain, you will be released. But the water of that fountain is being carried in the river, you don't have to take that water. You have to take the overflowing water.

After hearing all the words of Assad, the king brought water according to the king's description and fed it to the king. Assad was surprised to see the king. What a beautiful looking 55 year old man. And height as well. All the magic of King Aziz was released. At that time, the time of Assad's wrist clock was matching with the time of the palace clock. The color of the palace is changing. Gradually the palace is being destroyed. The fish in the river is decreasing. The river water is slowly drying up. All the green plains are slowly turning into hills. Then King Aziz and Assad are fleeing through the cave road. All the magic behind them is coming to be destroyed.

The king and Assad or Bashar al-Assad both escaped from the cave and left for Assad's house. On the way, Assad had the remaining two or four stones in his pocket, which he gave to the king for a closer look. He was startled to give the stones to the king. And he said it was no ordinary stone. Its name is diamond. This is the real diamond. Assad was upset to hear the king's words. He has unknowingly left many in the cave of sphere puzzles. The king fired back diamonds at Assad. The king stays at home for a while. Assad became rich by selling a couple of diamonds. He is a familiar person to the locals. At that time Akash stopped talking and went to sleep.

Iranian Nights 3

Eighth night.

Akash said, listen then today's story. The light began to lie down and listen to the story of the sky. Akash started telling stories and said listen to that story.

King Aziz will take Assad to the country of Venus with the permission of Assad's parents after staying in his family for some time. Locals suspect Assad's parents or his family. How their family became rich. A few days ago, Assad's father, Mohammed al-Basar, had to work hard to make ends meet. Meanwhile, King and Bashar al-Assad set out for Venice. After about a month, the king finally returned to the country. Then the palace and the people of the country burst into joy. Then Sultana Ileana leaves the throne to her father. The king appointed Bashar al-Assad Minister of Education and Finance. He is currently the new Minister of Venice, a good country. Assad's praise Qiyam or Venus has spread all over the country. Despite not being the king's prime minister, Assad got a fair trial with good advice. Qiyam set up a statue of Bashar al-Assad in the country's capital to rescue the king The king himself. Assad's honor is now at the top of the list. He took his parents to that country and started living there permanently. Assad's reputation is discussed everywhere. Unbeknownst to him, Sultana Ileana is thinking of Assad for love.

One day the Assad Department of Education suddenly decided that there would be separate high schools, colleges, and universities for all students. And all the poor students will get some money monthly. With which they will be able to meet their own needs for better education. Along with that there will be government vehicles for distant students. Will be able to travel in a small sense. Bashar al-Assad won the hearts of students from all over the world with this decision. As well as Sultana Eleanor. Why not, in the college where she is studying, Sultana Ileana's girlfriends used to praise Assad in front of the princess, but the princess once made up her mind. Moreover, Assad is a handsome and intelligent man. One day, Bashar al-Assad was passing by the princess's room and going to the king's room. The princess saw Bashar al-Assad as a minister and called him. Assad answered the prince's call and came to him and said, Adab will tell me something, Princess. Yes, there is something to be said. If you would give me a little time. Please tell, Princess. I need to go for a walk. We will go for a walk together. So I told him to take it.

After much thought, Assad said, "Okay, I'll go." That day came a few days later. He went on a journey with permission from King Aziz. One week trip. That trip is not as simple as the other five. Seven or eight people set out on a trip to Venice, a union territory of the country.

Everyone including the princess is going with joy. But while there is joy on everyone's face, there is no sign of joy on the face of Education and Finance Minister Assad. Everyone told him different things but he did not tell anyone on the way. After walking all day, he reached a house in the evening. The house is located in various flower and orchards. It is said to have been located in the middle of a beautiful flower and fruit park. High walls around the park. The park will feel more like a paradise at night than during the day. The party has been made more beautiful and dehumanized by the arrival of the princess and her companions. Even no one enters the park for a week. These were already matched by the princess. All the food menus will come from five star hotels in the state capital. Emergency service. The hotel is a little far away. So there is no problem from that. Gossip all day, Joy and travel. Arriving there, they were given their room number. Asad and Shahzadi's room fell side by side. Others were given different rooms. Everyone freshened up and sat down at the table to eat the royal food. Huge tall table. Everyone finished eating with joy. Half an hour after the meal, everyone went for a walk in the park. Then it was six o'clock at night. Even after nightfall, the park grounds are lit up. It never feels like night. On the banks of the river, that is, on the banks of the beautiful stone carvings, everyone is ready to hang their feet together and get involved in the story. Many are talking about Assad at the time. Assad understands not everything. At that moment, a friend smiled and said, Asad brother stand with the princess. Who will see how big. Who looks more beautiful. The princess smiled to herself. But Assad did not want to stand. The girlfriends forced the two of them to stand together. Then one of them said, wow, they both look very beautiful. Very agreeable. It would be nice if there was a way to hug you. The princess made eye contact with her friends and started pushing and shoving. Immediately the two began to push. The princess hugged Assad in the middle. Assad is shocked, he enters the room in shame and anger. The princess and her companions follow him. The princess goes to her room and sits stubbornly. Half of the princess's allies go in favor of the princess and Assad, and continue to persuade Assad. The princess loves him. He did not agree in any way. Assad wrote a letter to the king last night saying, The princess is bringing him here and proposing love. I don't want to stay here anymore. So I informed in advance. The king is thinking after reading the letter. Assad left the next day for the capital. The princess and her companions will come one day later. The next night he came to the king's room privately and handed over the resignation letter of the ministry to the king and said, "Dear uncle Shahjadi has offered me love." I know she is beautiful as a princess. I can fall in love with him because of his looks so my respect and respect and love for you may decrease. So after much thought I came to the conclusion that I want to live in another state with my family. Doing a business there will cover the expenses of the family. I am just going to another kingdom for my faith and my respect for you. The king was surprised to hear everything. He did not say anything to Assad but remained silent about the resignation letter. And he left the palace. The next day, Assad left the central capital and bought a house in a town in the state of Jaziya.

The princess is upset. There is no hunger. There is no joy in the palace. The king has no intention of doing anything. A matter of great concern. The prime minister and all members are accusing Assad of defamation and corruption. The king could not sit on the throne, but finally adjourned the meeting and went to the palace. The king was lying on the bed, obsessed with his thoughts. Think about the present. It was almost evening. Suddenly the king left for Assad's house. Alone he was leaving and finally reached home. However, when the vehicle arrived in disguise, he saluted and knocked on the door. A few minutes later, a middle-aged man appeared and opened the door. Then the king said I am the custodian of this city. The man was Assad's father taking the king inside and entertaining him. At that moment, Assad entered the market with vegetables. Everyone introduced. Then the king said, Dad, I have something to say to you. Assad took her to a separate room. Going to the room, the king gave his real identity to Assad. Assad is surprised. Then the king said, "Father, if you only think of yourself." Don't even think about us. How are we What am I doing? Saying this, the king started crying in front of Assad. Tears welled up in Assad's eyes, and he said, "I don't know who said that." I have come for your honor. As if you don't have to endure any slander from anyone. A notebook shows what Assad wrote about the king. Tears in the eyes of the king and Assad. Wiping away the water, the king said, "You go to the palace." Marry the princess. I never thought you were bad ' Asad's father. If you don't want to go, get married and stay here. I am giving you the responsibility of the state. Assad holds King's hand and cries and says I am not a high person. The princess will not agree with me. The tenants will say no bitter. Ordinary married to a person. Princess and you will not have respect. The king said, "I am announcing you as the Nawab or ruler of Jazira province from tomorrow." And you will make the current Nawab or ruler a minister. Finally, the king persuaded Assad to return to the palace. The princess calmed down a bit after her mother told her all the facts. At that moment, Akash stopped talking and fell asleep next to the light. I am announcing you as the Nawab or ruler of Jazira province from tomorrow. And you will make the current Nawab or ruler a minister. Finally, the king persuaded Assad to return to the palace. The princess calmed down a bit after her mother told her all the facts. At that moment, Akash stopped talking and fell asleep next to the light. I am announcing you as the Nawab or ruler of Jazira province from tomorrow. And you will make the current Nawab or ruler a minister. Finally, the king persuaded Assad to return to the palace. The princess calmed down a bit after her mother told her all the facts. At that moment, Akash stopped talking and fell asleep next to the light.

Navratri

A few days later, Assad was elected Nawab of Jaziyah province. The former Nawab of Jaziyah province has been appointed prime minister of Rakhine state. The education and finance departments in the former Nawab's kingdom of Jaziyah province did not have good infrastructure. Assad is currently a Nawab. Meanwhile, the princess is waiting for the wedding. The princess sent a letter to Nawab Bashar al-Assad. It is as if he had a private meeting in Nayanmani House. Assad also fell in love, but too late. The only reason for that is called the king's daughter. Moreover, Assad is also not eligible to leave. As a result of sexual arousal and intercourse with the eyes, women are more or less intoxicated in his eyes. And like a beautiful lady from the eyes, Kampurna and Danakata fairy. The girl's luck is really good. She was not married to the king's ex-son-in-law. But in my mind, Assad's tension has risen. Before he left, he stood in front of the mirror wearing a nice pants-shirt, applied a light perfume and tidied his hair. The king and queen are discussing their marriage. After the marriage of the princess will deal with the enemies. Later, Qiyam ruled by Sultan Salauddin's minister declared war on the country. King Aziz promised Begum that he would change everything gradually.

Bashar al-Assad, the son-in-law of the king, the independent Nawab of Jaziyah province, finally arrived at Nayanmani House. It is only the private housing of princes and princesses. Where no one has access without their permission. There is no one in the housing except the princess. And the staff with some soldiers and feudal lords are also out of the main housing again. They have completely different arrangements. However, the guards at the main gate greeted Bashar al-Assad as soon as he entered. Princess Sultana Ileana is sitting in front of the mirror, dressing herself. She is wearing a light pink sari blouse. Even slightly swollen breasts can be seen. Glass bangles in hand. Everything is pink today. Just look like the queen of sex. Ileana has never had a sex partner. No one in this life has touched youth. Lean body. Ileana to see Ileana by name. Sitting in front of the mirror, looking at himself again and again, how he feels. Such The time came for Assad to shake his head. Ileana laughed softly and said, "What's the matter, Mr. so late?" Late where my darling.

Lately, he sat down on the front sofa. At that time a female employee came with breakfast. The girl left with a snack. Ileana closed the door of the room by herself. Assad just wiped his hands after drinking milk. Ileana pushed the food cart to one side of the table. Assad lay down on the bed and Eliana lay on Assad's chest unbuttoning his shirt one by one. The young age of the two. Ileana will probably be eighteen and Assad will be nineteen or twenty. Ileana started kissing Assad's lips and there was a feeling of electricity in Assad's body. Ileana's agitated body is making Assad more aroused. A few minutes later, as Assad's excitement reached its climax, Ileana lay down on the bed with her neck down. The lips and the navel of the abdomen began to kiss strongly. Ileana is growling. After a while, the two of them took a break from it and a feeling of laughter and joy began to appear in their youth. At that moment, Akash stopped talking and turned off the light and fell asleep.

Iranian Nights 4

Eighth night.

Akash said, listen then today's story. The light began to lie down and listen to the story of the sky. Akash started telling stories and said listen to that story.

King Aziz will take Assad to the country of Venus with the permission of Assad's parents after staying in his family for some time. Locals suspect Assad's parents or his family. How their family became rich. A few days ago, Assad's father, Mohammed al-Basar, had to work hard to make ends meet. Meanwhile, King and Bashar al-Assad set out for Venice. After about a month, the king finally returned to the country. Then the palace and the people of the country burst into joy. Then Sultana Ileana leaves the throne to her father. The king appointed Bashar al-Assad Minister of Education and Finance. He is currently the new Minister of Venice, a good country. Assad's praise Qiyam or Venus has spread all over the country. Despite not being the king's prime minister, Assad got a fair trial with good advice. Qiyam set up a statue of Bashar al-Assad in the country's capital to rescue the king The king himself. Assad's honor is now at the top of the list. He took his parents to that country and started living there permanently. Assad's reputation is discussed everywhere. Unbeknownst to him, Sultana Ileana is thinking of Assad for love.

One day the Assad Department of Education suddenly decided that there would be separate high schools, colleges, and universities for all students. And all the poor students will get some money monthly. With which they will be able to meet their own needs for better education. Along with that there will be government vehicles for distant students. Will be able to travel in a small sense. Bashar al-Assad won the hearts of students from all over the world with this decision. As well as Sultana Eleanor. Why not, in the college where she is studying, Sultana Ileana's girlfriends used to praise Assad in front of the princess, but the princess once made up her mind. Moreover, Assad is a handsome and intelligent man. One day, Bashar al-Assad was passing by the princess's room and going to the king's room. The princess saw Bashar al-Assad as a minister and called him. Assad answered the prince's call and came to him and said, Adab will tell me something, Princess. Yes, there is something to be said. If you would give me a little time. Please tell, Princess. I need to go for a walk. We will go for a walk together. So I told him to take it.

After much thought, Assad said, "Okay, I'll go." That day came a few days later. He went on a journey with permission from King Aziz. One week trip. That trip is not as simple as the other five. Seven or eight people set out on a trip to Venice, a union territory of the country.

Everyone including the princess is going with joy. But while there is joy on everyone's face, there is no sign of joy on the face of Education and Finance Minister Assad. Everyone told him different things but he did not tell anyone on the way. After walking all day, he reached a house in the evening. The house is located in various flower and orchards. It is said to have been located in the middle of a beautiful flower and fruit park. High walls around the park. The park will feel more like a paradise at night than during the day. The party has been made more beautiful and dehumanized by the arrival of the princess and her companions. Even no one enters the park for a week. These were already matched by the princess. All the food menus will come from five star hotels in the state capital. Emergency service. The hotel is a little far away. So there is no problem from that. Gossip all day, Joy and travel. Arriving there, they were given their room number. Asad and Shahzadi's room fell side by side. Others were given different rooms. Everyone freshened up and sat down at the table to eat the royal food. Huge tall table. Everyone finished eating with joy. Half an hour after the meal, everyone went for a walk in the park. Then it was six o'clock at night. Even after nightfall, the park grounds are lit up. It never feels like night. On the banks of the river, that is, on the banks of the beautiful stone carvings, everyone is ready to hang their feet together and get involved in the story. Many are talking about Assad at the time. Assad understands not everything. At that moment, a friend smiled and said, Asad brother stand with the princess. Who will see how big. Who looks more beautiful. The princess smiled to herself. But Assad did not want to stand. The girlfriends forced the two of them to stand together. Then one of them said, wow, they both look very beautiful. Very agreeable. It would be nice if there was a way to hug you. The princess made eye contact with her friends and started pushing and shoving. Immediately the two began to push. The princess hugged Assad in the middle. Assad is shocked, he enters the room in shame and anger. The princess and her companions follow him. The princess goes to her room and sits stubbornly. Half of the princess's allies go in favor of the princess and Assad, and continue to persuade Assad. The princess loves him. He did not agree in any way. Assad wrote a letter to the king last night saying, The princess is bringing him here and proposing love. I don't want to stay here anymore. So I informed in advance. The king is thinking after reading the letter. Assad left the next day for the capital. The princess and her companions will come one day later. The next night he came to the king's room privately and handed over the resignation letter of the ministry to the king and said, "Dear uncle Shahjadi has offered me love." I know she is beautiful as a princess. I can fall in love with him because of his looks so my respect and respect and love for you may decrease. So after much thought I came to the conclusion that I want to live in another state with my family. Doing a business there will cover the expenses of the family. I am just going to another kingdom for my faith and my respect for you. The king was surprised to hear everything. He did not say anything to Assad but remained silent about the resignation letter. And he left the palace. The next day, Assad left the central capital and bought a house in a town in the state of Jaziya.

The princess is upset. There is no hunger. There is no joy in the palace. The king has no intention of doing anything. A matter of great concern. The prime minister and all members are accusing Assad of defamation and corruption. The king could not sit on the throne, but finally adjourned the meeting and went to the palace. The king was lying on the bed, obsessed with his thoughts. Think about the present. It was almost evening. Suddenly the king left for Assad's house. Alone he was leaving and finally reached home. However, when the vehicle arrived in disguise, he saluted and knocked on the door. A few minutes later, a middle-aged man appeared and opened the door. Then the king said I am the custodian of this city. The man was Assad's father taking the king inside and entertaining him. At that moment, Assad entered the market with vegetables. Everyone introduced. Then the king said, Dad, I have something to say to you. Assad took her to a separate room. Going to the room, the king gave his real identity to Assad. Assad is surprised. Then the king said, "Father, if you only think of yourself." Don't even think about us. How are we What am I doing? Saying this, the king started crying in front of Assad. Tears welled up in Assad's eyes, and he said, "I don't know who said that." I have come for your honor. As if you don't have to endure any slander from anyone. A notebook shows what Assad wrote about the king. Tears in the eyes of the king and Assad. Wiping away the water, the king said, "You go to the palace." Marry the princess. I never thought you were bad ' Asad's father. If you don't want to go, get married and stay here. I am giving you the responsibility of the state. Assad holds King's hand and cries and says I am not a high person. The princess will not agree with me. The tenants will say no bitter. Ordinary married to a person. Princess and you will not have respect. The king said, "I am announcing you as the Nawab or ruler of Jazira province from tomorrow." And you will make the current Nawab or ruler a minister. Finally, the king persuaded Assad to return to the palace. The princess calmed down a bit after her mother told her all the facts. At that moment, Akash stopped talking and fell asleep next to the light. I am announcing you as the Nawab or ruler of Jazira province from tomorrow. And you will make the current Nawab or ruler a minister. Finally, the king persuaded Assad to return to the palace. The princess calmed down a bit after her mother told her all the facts. At that moment, Akash stopped talking and fell asleep next to the light. I am announcing you as the Nawab or ruler of Jazira province from tomorrow. And you will make the current Nawab or ruler a minister. Finally, the king persuaded Assad to return to the palace. The princess calmed down a bit after her mother told her all the facts. At that moment, Akash stopped talking and fell asleep next to the light.

Navratri

A few days later, Assad was elected Nawab of Jaziyah province. The former Nawab of Jaziyah province has been appointed prime minister of Rakhine state. The education and finance departments in the former Nawab's kingdom of Jaziyah province did not have good infrastructure. Assad is currently a Nawab. Meanwhile, the princess is waiting for the wedding. The princess sent a letter to Nawab Bashar al-Assad. It is as if he had a private meeting in Nayanmani House. Assad also fell in love, but too late. The only reason for that is called the king's daughter. Moreover, Assad is also not eligible to leave. As a result of sexual arousal and intercourse with the eyes, women are more or less intoxicated in his eyes. And like a beautiful lady from the eyes, Kampurna and Danakata fairy. The girl's luck is really good. She was not married to the king's ex-son-in-law. But in my mind, Assad's tension has risen. Before he left, he stood in front of the mirror wearing a nice pants-shirt, applied a light perfume and tidied his hair. The king and queen are discussing their marriage. After the marriage of the princess will deal with the enemies. Later, Qiyam ruled by Sultan Salauddin's minister declared war on the country. King Aziz promised Begum that he would change everything gradually.

Bashar al-Assad, the son-in-law of the king, the independent Nawab of Jaziyah province, finally arrived at Nayanmani House. It is only the private housing of princes and princesses. Where no one has access without their permission. There is no one in the housing except the princess. And the staff with some soldiers and feudal lords are also out of the main housing again. They have completely different arrangements. However, the guards at the main gate greeted Bashar al-Assad as soon as he entered. Princess Sultana Ileana is sitting in front of the mirror, dressing herself. She is wearing a light pink sari blouse. Even slightly swollen breasts can be seen. Glass bangles in hand. Everything is pink today. Just look like the queen of sex. Ileana has never had a sex partner. No one in this life has touched youth. Lean body. Ileana to see Ileana by name. Sitting in front of the mirror, looking at himself again and again, how he feels. Such The time came for Assad to shake his head. Ileana laughed softly and said, "What's the matter, Mr. so late?" Late where my darling.

Lately, he sat down on the front sofa. At that time a female employee came with breakfast. The girl left with a snack. Ileana closed the door of the room by herself. Assad just wiped his hands after drinking milk. Ileana pushed the food cart to one side of the table. Assad lay down on the bed and Eliana lay on Assad's chest unbuttoning his shirt one by one. The young age of the two. Ileana will probably be eighteen and Assad will be nineteen or twenty. Ileana started kissing Assad's lips and there was a feeling of electricity in Assad's body. Ileana's agitated body is making Assad more aroused. A few minutes later, as Assad's excitement reached its climax, Ileana lay down on the bed with her neck down. The lips and the navel of the abdomen began to kiss strongly. Ileana is growling. After a while, the two of them took a break from it and a feeling of laughter and joy began to appear in their youth. At that moment, Akash stopped talking and turned off the light and fell asleep.

Iranian Nights 5

The eleventh night

King Aziz and Sultan Assad were worried. How to cross is not a one or two step road, it will be about fifty feet road. King Aziz said it was impossible, but the elder brother knew how to go. That too is a matter of concern. Looking around for clues. Searching, they finally found a stone inscription. The text is as follows,

"Match your locket,
In the groove of the buttocks in the groove of the saw.
Cross the wide road,
In a few minutes. "

After Asad found the rock, he showed it to King Aziz. The king read and understood what Sultan Salauddin meant. The locket is actually the key to the street. Sultan Salauddin used to cross it. The two of them started looking for the key matching key. Looking around. As soon as the groove was finally found, the locket was put in the groove and it was seen that the two-inch iron saw road became ten to twelve feet wide. King Aziz and Bashar al-Assad started walking down that road. After the road was cleared, all those caves were filled with light like daylight. As soon as the two crossed, the road closed again as before. Assad was frightened, but King Aziz put his hand on his back and said, "Don't be afraid, father." Look, there is a key groove here too. On the way back, the road will be opened only if the locket is matched in the groove. Assad was relieved by his father-in-law's assurance. They slowly reached a huge room. They were shocked to see that. So many big rooms inside the mountain cave. They could not imagine. The design shows that the treasury and the treasury are below. King Aziz is looking for. The exact design of the map was found while searching. There is also information on how to use the design. In simple language, of course. Such a sunflower on an iron plate. A horse's face on him. That, of course, is iron. There's a key notch. The door will open as soon as the key is matched there. As soon as the locket was matched in a groove, an iron cross mark came. Turning it twice to the right and turning it to the left, the door of the underworld opened on the huge empty floor. From there the stone stairs went down. The room was as clean as day. King Aziz and Assad to get down Looked like. After descending, he finally reached Patalpuri. I came there and saw a huge door of high quality. So that there is no lock and key system. There is only one chain. According to the description of the locked key, the king started looking for it. It is said that there is a circle in front of the door. You have to stand there and walk fourteen hands on the right. You have to stand there again and walk three hands to the left. And if you stand there, you will see an iron chain. As soon as you pull the chain, an iron box will come. That box will have the key to the chain lock. What he saw after opening the lock after receiving the key is unbelievable. It was found that the room is full of different types of gold and silver gems from floor to ceiling. There are also native sultani coins. With which the country of Qiyam Desh will be ruled by the people for thousands of years. There is a circle in front of the door. You have to stand there and walk fourteen hands on the right. You have to stand there again and walk three hands to the left. And if you stand there, you will see an iron chain. As soon as you pull the chain, an iron box will come. That box will have the key to the chain lock. What he saw after unlocking the key was unbelievable. It was found that the room is full of different types of gold and silver gems from floor to ceiling. There are also native sultani coins. With which the country of Qiyam Desh will be ruled by the people for thousands of years.

The chamber was about fifty feet long and thirty feet wide. The two of them returned to the palace with five sacks of coins and various gems. However, the cave door has come through as it was before.

At that moment, Akash saw that his wife, Alo, had fallen asleep. So he stopped talking and lay down on the bed.

Fourteenth night

The king left for a few days in his own country. Meanwhile, Begum and Sultan Bashar al-Assad did not get any opportunity to express their love as Ileana had parents. It has not become possible to go anywhere with it. After marriage, they did not go anywhere due to work pressure. To beautify the country's financial system. Sultana Assad would not agree to go anywhere, finally agreed in the evening. He told Sultana that he could travel in disguise in the city park. As usual, he went out to walk in the park in a very simple way. Go to a VIP restaurant and eat expensive foreign food. Went to the library. I watched movies for a while. He bought some beautiful things and returned to the palace. It will be about ten o'clock at night. Nothing like that night in town. Sultan Asad came to his room at night and slept in the warehouse. Begum came to change her sari but saw that she was still lying. Begum Ileana insisted and said let's take a bath in the wash room. Begum Ileana has brought clothes for both of them. Why not take a bath. How many germs are there in the body when you go for a walk on a hot night. Forced to take a bath in the swimming pool.

Assad was knocked out and Begum Ileana fell. Assad was sitting in a water chair under the swimming pool. There, Ileana sat hugging Assad's body with the same face. The two looked very pretty when wet in the water. More to Ileana. Because Sultana is wearing a thin short skirt. There is nothing left in the body of Asad wearing Bengali lungi. Pale, muscular body. Who wouldn't like. No matter what the girls say, the power of cum is more important for the girls. Cum arousal is coming despite having wet bodies of more than two. Thinking like this, he suddenly came forward, picked up Ileana on his lap, grabbed Bashar al-Assad and started kissing her. There is no body space left to kiss, even up to the lips throat navel abdomen. Premlila has been going on for about half an hour. Finally the two of them returned to the room after bathing with

joy. Ileana's arousal is so great that, Probably impossible for anyone without Assad. God sent it right. It's true Ileana has never shared youthful irritation with anyone in her life. In this way their luxurious life continued. Sultan Assad used to be nice to his subjects. They are by their side in danger.
One day, Sultan Bashar al-Assad's generals and spies were captured. They were hanged. The only prince, King Aziz, released the eldest son and sent him back to the country. All the wealth of the bandits was confiscated by Sultan Bashar al-Assad. The commander-in-chief and the spy were appointed governors of two separate provinces. Qiyam was liberated and Sultana Asad was able to run the country smoothly.

While telling the story, Akash saw that his wife told Alo that I know a better story than this. Alo began to plead for telling the story. In the way of cum arousal. The eyes of light were then great youthful excitement. Akash hugged and kissed the back of the light to tell the story tomorrow. The two of them woke up many nights and fell asleep after performing Premlila's feat.

www.ingramcontent.com/pod-product-compliance
Lightning Source LLC
LaVergne TN
LVHW050427160726
843469LV00041B/1254
* 9 7 8 9 3 5 6 1 0 4 5 5 6 *